Edward Everett, Edward E. Hale, Alexander Hill Everett

Cuba

The Everett Letters on Cuba

Edward Everett, Edward E. Hale, Alexander Hill Everett

Cuba
The Everett Letters on Cuba

ISBN/EAN: 9783337379247

Printed in Europe, USA, Canada, Australia, Japan

Cover: Foto ©Andreas Hilbeck / pixelio.de

More available books at **www.hansebooks.com**

THE

EVERETT LETTERS

ON

CUBA

BOSTON

Geo. H. Ellis, Printer, 141 Franklin Street

1897

PREFACE.

These two letters are of such importance in the discussions of to-day that it seems desirable to reprint them.

Alexander Hill Everett, our minister to Spain from the year 1825 to 1829, was commissioned by Mr. John Quincy Adams on his election to the presidency. Mr. Clay was the Secretary of State who gave to Mr. Everet, his commission. It should be remembered that Mr. Everett had served under Mr. Adams almost from his boyhood, having been an under-secretary at St. Petersburg as early as 1809. These personal relations with Mr. Adams make it well-nigh certain that the conversation which is described in this letter took place at Mr. Adams's personal suggestion. A trained diplomatist like Mr. Everett would never have ventured on this conversation unless he were sure of the approval of Mr. Adams and Mr. Clay. Here is one indication, among many which will occur to the well-informed reader, that the traditions of our foreign policy, for much more than

4

half a century, have looked in the direction of a certain protectorate over Cuba. A protectorate over Cuba in no sort means the annexation of Cuba as a constituent part of our government.

When, in 1852, two or three of the great powers proposed to the United States, in an amiable way, that she should join them in guaranteeing the Spanish government of Cuba, Mr. Edward Everett was fortunately in the Department of State. The insidious proposal made to us then was met by the second letter here published.

EDWARD E. HALE.

[From Scribner's Monthly, April, 1876.]

CUBA WITHOUT WAR.

LETTER FROM ALEXANDER H. EVERETT TO THE PRESIDENT OF THE UNITED STATES.

MADRID, Nov. 30, 1825.

DEAR SIR,—I think it proper to make you acquainted with one circumstance in my intercourse with this Government of rather a delicate nature which I have not introduced into my despatches on account of their being liable to be called for and published at any moment. It occurred in my communications with the Minister* upon our relations with the island of Cuba.

It has always appeared to me, and such I believe is the general opinion in the United States, that this island forms properly an appendage of the Floridas. Since the cession of these provinces † an impression has generally prevailed throughout the country that Cuba must at one time or another belong to us. Indeed, this idea was entertained, as I have been told, by many persons of the highest respectability, including Mr. Jefferson, long

---

*The Minister, at the date of this note, was the Duke del Infantado, who had been appointed a few weeks before. But the Minister referred to in the text was Zea Bermudez, the duke's predecessor.

† This cession was made by Spain in a treaty concluded in October, 1820.

before the conclusion of the Florida treaty. It grows naturally out of a consideration of the Geographical position of the island as respects the United States. In the hands of a powerful and active nation, it would carry with it so complete a control over the commerce of the Gulph of Mexico, and over the navigation of the River Mississippi, as to endanger very much the intercourse of our country in that quarter. Our safety from this danger has, I believe, long been considered as resulting wholly from the feebleness and insufficiency of Spain; and it has been viewed by all as a settled point that the American Government could not consent to any change in the political situation of Cuba other than one which should place it under the jurisdiction of the United States. This view of the subject is strongly intimated in my official instructions. Such are the first considerations that present themselves in regard to our relations with the island of Cuba. The next in order are that it is impossible, in fact,— in consequence of the internal state of the island, the obstinate adherence of Spain to the Colonial System, and the growing strength of the new States,— that the island can remain in its present situation. It may be assumed as certain that the war will be continued by Spain for an indefinite period. Half a century may very probably elapse before she recognizes the independence of the colonies.* On the other hand, it is quite evident, and such is the opin-

---

*In fact, the independence of Mexico was not recognized by Spain till Dec. 28, 1836.

ion of the Government as expressed in my instructions, that, as long as the war is kept up, the situation of the island is in the highest degree precarious, that it is liable to be changed every year, every month even, and that it cannot remain as it is more than two or three years. The white inhabitants form too small a proportion of the whole number to constitute of themselves an independent State. The island, therefore, must assume, whenever it changes its present condition, one of two others. It must either fall into the hands of some power different from Spain, as probably Mexico or Columbia, or it must become an independent principality of blacks. Neither part of this alternative can be considered as admissible; and a view of our present relations with the island presents, therefore, the following results : —

1st. The situation of the island must inevitably be changed within two or three years, and may be changed at any moment.

2d. No change can possibly occur without the intervention of the United States which they could regard as admissible.

From these premises, it seems to follow, as a necessary conclusion, that it is the policy and duty of the United States to endeavor to obtain possession of the island immediately in a peaceable way. If they do not succeed in this, it is morally certain that they will be forced, at no very distant period, to effect the same object in a more invidious manner, and at the risk of embroiling themselves with some of the great powers of Europe. The principal question, therefore, is whether any consideration could be presented to the Spanish ministry of a nature to induce them to cede the island. If this were possible, it would appear to be the policy of the United States to commence the negotiation without delay. Viewing the subject in this light, and recollecting at the same time the great financial embarrassments under which this Government is now laboring, it has occurred to me that the offer of a considerable loan, on condition of a temporary cession of the island in deposit as security for the payment of it, would be as likely to succeed as any proposition that could be made upon the subject. The interest might be made payable out of the revenues of the island, which are said to amount to between four and five millions of dollars; * and, if the money were not paid within a pretty long limited time, complete sovereignty might vest in the United States. Considering the character of the Spanish Government, and their general system of administration, a cession of this kind, accompanied with an immediate delivery of possession, would be equivalent, as respects us, to a direct cession of the whole sovereignty. In the view of the Spanish Government, it might perhaps wear a more agreeable aspect. It would present to them the two following great advantages : —

1st. The obtaining of a loan sufficient to meet their im-

* The revenues of Cuba are now supposed [1876] to be twenty millions of dollars.

mediate wants on good terms,— a thing which seems to be absolutely indispensable, which there is apparently no possibility of effecting in any other way, on any terms, and which, if in reality effected in any other way, must be a transaction, prudentially considered, of the most desperate character. This advantage is by no means a light one, since it seems impossible even to imagine how this Government can get along six months without new resources.

2d. The second advantage would be the assurance of retaining the island in the event of repaying the loan. Whatever confidence this Government may affect in the results of their colonial system, it is impossible that they should not be aware to a certain extent of the great danger to which they are exposed of losing the islands.* They may not be so fully satisfied, as most foreigners probably are, of the moral impossibility that they would be able to pay down fifteen or twenty millions of dollars twenty years hence, and might, therefore, regard a transaction of this kind as considerably increasing their assurance of a continued possession of Cuba. Such, in fact, would be the probable effect of it, if we suppose the Spanish Government, notwithstanding their affected determination *never* to surrender their rights, to intend, nevertheless, in secret, to recognize the colonies after a few years, should things go on in their present course. Supposing this to be their policy, they would obtain, by ceding the island to us in the way I have suggested, a

* Cuba and Porto Rico.

complete assurance of the continued possession of it from the moment when the delivery to the United States was effected. This temporary transfer would secure it from the danger of attack or internal convulsion while it lasted; and, upon the recognition of the colonies, Spain would without difficulty obtain from them a much larger indemnity in money than would be necessary to ransom the island. It is not, however, probable that Spain now intends to recognize the colonies at no very distant period, and I have already assumed that she does not. These considerations might, nevertheless, be presented to her, and, being extremely obvious and cogent, might perhaps make an impression.

But, supposing this Government, as I do, to be completely resolved upon adhering to their system, and yet aware of the danger of losing the island, and of the impossibility of ever repaying a loan of the kind mentioned without recognizing the colonies, they might yet think it better to get twenty millions for the island than to lose it for nothing.

Such are the advantages of the transaction as respects 'Spain. As respects the United States, it holds out the two following, which are so obvious that I need not enlarge upon them : —

1st. Complete security from the danger of any change in the position of the island in consequence of the present troubles.

2d. The probability of an eventual acquisition of the entire sovereignty.

It may perhaps be thought that some of the great foreign powers, particularly England or France, would take umbrage at the acquisition by us of the sovereignty of Cuba; that the probability of this ought to prevent us from taking any measure to obtain it; and that it would, at any rate, hinder Spain from ceding it to us directly or indirectly.

The weight of this objection you are, of course, better able to appreciate than I am. It does not strike me that the foreign powers ought to feel, or would, in fact, feel, the same repugnance to our occupying Cuba as we should to their doing it; and, if we consider the acquisition of the island by a peaceable transaction as the only means of avoiding the necessity of taking possession of it sooner or later by force,— which is the view I have taken of the subject,— it is evident that the repugnance of the foreign powers, whatever it may be, is no real objection, because it must in the end be met. They would probably be much more dissatisfied to see us occupy the island by force than to see us acquire it by purchase.

These considerations appear to me to recommend very powerfully the policy of endeavoring to acquire the island of Cuba in a peaceable way; and the manner I have indicated seems the one which would be the most likely to succeed. I should not, of course, think of making any formal proposition on the subject without receiving your instructions ; and, should the suggestions I have now made appear to be of a nature to be acted on seriously, you will have the goodness to favor me with your orders, either through the Department of State or in a private letter, as you may think most expedient. I have thought, however, that there would be no impropriety in sounding the intentions of the Government beforehand in an informal way; and I accordingly took an opportunity of doing it in one of the conversations I had with Mr. Zea. After some remarks on both sides on the financial difficulties of the country and the necessity of obtaining a loan, if possible, from some quarter, I told him that, although I had not the slightest authority to offer any proposition of the kind, I thought it not improbable that the Government of the United States would make a considerable loan to that of Spain, and on favorable terms, on condition that Spain would consent to a temporary cession in deposit of the island of Cuba, accompanied with a delivery of possession; and I then stated to him some of the advantages of such a transaction to the two parties, as recapitulated above. He did not, of course, give his assent to the proposal, but, on the contrary, expressed the opinion that the king would not alienate the island for a moment on any consideration whatever. I did not, however, consider this answer as at all decisive. A transaction of this sort would naturally require great consideration in all its stages; and the only safe and proper mode of treating the subject in the first instance would be that of a refusal. I saw that my remarks had made a pretty strong impression on Mr. Zea. He said that, if I had authority to make a proposition of this kind, he should be glad to receive it in writing. I told him in answer to this that the suggestion was entirely private and personal, that I had no instructions from you to make it; that the transaction appeared to me so advantageous to both Governments that I had ventured to advise it without knowing whether it would be agreeable to either; but that, if the king approved of the proposition, I would immediately write home, and recommend the adoption of it for the reasons which I had already summarily stated.

I have since been informed in a private way that Mr. Zea took a written note of what I said. This conversation passed during the last interview I had with him. I learn that the Duke del Infantado found these notes among Mr. Zea's papers, and concluded from them that a serious negotiation was actually going on for the cession of Cuba. I have not yet said anything to the Duke upon the subject, but shall perhaps take an opportunity of mentioning it, and of ascertaining whether the proposition is regarded by this Government as at all plausible. I shall carefully keep you informed of any such communications that I may have with the Minister, and will thank you to instruct me whether you wish the matter to be pressed seriously or dropped altogether. It struck me that it would be agreeable to you to learn without any commitment whatever of the Government in what way a proposal of this kind would be received and treated upon its first suggestion.

I have given you in my despatches a full account of

the progress of the negotiations with which I am charged. They are still in an incipient state; but the present appearance of them is not unfavorable. Should this Government, however, attempt to proceed upon its usual plan of delay, after all that has already passed, I cannot but hope that Congress will resort to vigorous measures. The mere demonstration would in this case be effectual, and would be unattended with any danger or inconvenience whatever. Nevertheless, violence is always unpleasant, even when necessary, politic, and safe, so that I should prefer an early termination of these vexatious disputes in an amicable way. It shall not be for want of attention on my part if this result does not happen.

I have the honor to be, dear sir, with much respect, your very sincere friend and obedient servant,

ALEXANDER H. EVERETT.

MR. EVERETT TO THE COMTE DE SARTIGES.

DEPARTMENT OF STATE,
WASHINGTON, December 1, 1852.

SIR: You are well acquainted with the melancholy circumstances which have hitherto prevented a reply to the note which you addressed to my predecessor on the 8th of July.

That note, and the instruction of M. de Turgot of the 31st March, with a similar communication from the English Minister, and the *projet* of a convention between the three powers relative to Cuba, have been among the first subjects to which my attention has been called by the President.

The substantial portion of the proposed convention is expressed in a single article in the following terms: "The high contracting parties hereby severally and collectively disclaim now and for hereafter, all intention to obtain possession of the island of Cuba, and they respectively bind themselves to discountenance all attempt to that effect on the part of any power or individuals whatever."

"The high contracting parties declare, severally and collectively, that they will not obtain or maintain for themselves, or for any one of themselves, any exclusive control over the said island, nor assume nor exercise any dominion over the same."

The President has given the most serious attention to this proposal, to the notes of the French and British ministers accompanying it, and to the instructions of M. de Turgot and the Earl of Malmesbury, transmitted with the project of the convention; and he directs me to make known to you the view which he takes of this important and delicate subject.

The President fully concurs with his predecessors, who have on more than one occasion authorized the declaration referred to by M. de Turgot and Lord Malmesbury, that the United States could not see with indifference the island of Cuba fall into possession of any other European government than Spain; not, however, because we should be dissatisfied with any natural increase of territory and power on the part of France or England. France has, within twenty years, acquired a vast domain on the northern coast of Africa, with a fair prospect of indefinite extension. England, within a half century, has added very extensively to her empire. These acquisitions have created no uneasiness on the part of the United States.

In like manner, the United States have, within the same period, greatly increased their territory. The largest addition was that of Louisiana, which was purchased from France. These accessions of territory have probably caused no uneasiness to the great European powers, as they have been brought about by the operation of natural causes, and without any disturbance of the international relations of the principal States. They have been followed, also, by a great increase of mutually beneficial commercial intercourse between the United States and Europe.

But the case would be different in reference to the transfer of Cuba from Spain to any other European power. That event could not take place without a serious derangement of the international system now existing, and it would indicate designs in reference to this hemisphere which could not but awaken alarm in the United States.

We should view it in somewhat the same light in which France and England would view the acquisition of some important island in the Mediterranean by the United States, with this difference, it is true : that the attempt of the United States to establish themselves in Europe would be a novelty, while the appearance of a European power in this part of the world is a familiar fact. But this difference in the two cases is merely historical, and would not diminish the anxiety which, on political grounds, would be caused by any great demonstration of European power in a new direction in America.

M. de Turgot states that France could never see with indifference the possession of Cuba by *any* power but

Spain, and explicitly declares that she has no wish or intention of appropriating the island to herself; and the English minister makes the some avowal on behalf of his government. M. de Turgot and Lord Malmesbury do the government of the United States no more than justice in remarking that they have often pronounced themselves substantially in the same sense. The President does not covet the acquisition of Cuba for the United States; at the same time, he considers the condition of Cuba as mainly an American question. The proposed convention proceeds on a different principle. It assumes that the United States have no other or greater interest in the question than France or England; whereas it is necessary only to cast one's eye on the map to see how remote are the relations of Europe, and how intimate those of the United States, with this island.

The President, doing full justice to the friendly spirit in which his concurrence is invited by France and England, and not insensible to the advantages of a good understanding between the three powers in reference to Cuba, feels himself, nevertheless, unable to become a party to the proposed compact, for the following reasons:

It is, in the first place, in his judgment, clear (as far as the respect due from the Executive to a coördinate branch of the government will permit him to anticipate its decision) that no such convention would be viewed with favor by the Senate. Its certain rejection by that body would leave the question of Cuba in a more unsettled position than it is now. This objection would not require the President to withhold his concurrence from the convention if no other objection existed, and if a strong sense of the utility of the measure rendered it his duty, as far as the Executive action is concerned, to give his consent to the arrangement. Such, however, is not the case.

The convention would be of no value unless it were lasting: accordingly, its terms express a perpetuity of purpose and obligation. Now, it may well be doubted whether the constitution of the United States would allow the treaty-making power to impose a permanent disability on the American government, for all coming time, and prevent it, under any future change of circumstances, from doing what has been so often done in times past. In 1803 the United States purchased Louisiana of France; and in 1819 they purchased Florida of Spain. It is not within the competence of the treaty-making power in 1852 effectually to bind the government in all its branches; and, for all coming time, not to make a similar purchase of Cuba. A like remark, I imagine, may be made even in reference both to France and England, where the treaty-making power is less subject than it is with us to the control of other branches of the government.

There is another strong objection to the proposed

agreement. Among the oldest traditions of the federal government is an aversion to political alliances with European powers. In his memorable farewell address, President Washington says : "The great rule of conduct for us in regard to foreign nations is, in extending our commercial relations, to have with them as little political connection as possible. So far as we have already formed engagements, let them be fulfilled with perfect good faith. Here let us stop." President Jefferson in his inaugural address, in 1801, warned the country against "entangling alliances." This expression, now become proverbial, was unquestionably used by Mr. Jefferson in reference with the alliance with France of 1778—an alliance, at the time, of incalculable benefit to the United States; but which, in less than twenty years, came near involving us in the wars of the French revolution, and laid the foundation of heavy claims upon Congress, not extinguished to the present day. It is a significant coincidence, that the particular provision of the alliance which occasioned these evils was that, under which France called upon us to aid her in defending her West Indian possessions against England. Nothing less than the unbounded influence of Washington rescued the Union from the perils of that crisis, and preserved our neutrality.

But the President has a graver objection to entering into the proposed convention. He has no wish to disguise the feeling that the compact, although equal in

its terms, would be very unequal in substance. France
and England, by entering into it, would disable themselves from obtaining possession of an island remote
from their seats of government, belonging to another
European power, whose natural right to possess it must
always be as good as their own—a distant island in another hemisphere, and one by which no ordinary or
peaceful course of things could ever belong to either of
them. If the present balance of power in Europe
should be broken up, if Spain should become unable to
maintain the island in her possession, and France and
England should be engaged in a death struggle with
each other, Cuba might then be the prize of the victor.
Till these events all take place, the President does not
see how Cuba can belong to any European power but
Spain.

The United States, on the other hand, would, by the
proposed convention, disable themselves from making
an acquisition which might take place without any disturbance of existing foreign relations, and in the natural order of things. The island of Cuba lies at our
doors. It commands the approach to the Gulf of Mexico, which washes the shores of five of our States. It
bars the entrance of that great river which drains half
the North American continent, and with its tributaries
forms the largest system of internal water-communica-
tion in the world. It keeps watch at the doorway of
our intercourse with California by the isthmus route.

If an island like Cuba, belonging to the Spanish crown, guarded the entrance of the Thames and the Seine, and the United States should propose a convention like this to France and England, those powers would assuredly feel that the disability assumed by ourselves was far less serious than that which we asked them to assume.

The opinions of American statesmen, at different times, and under varying circumstances, have differed as to the desirableness of the acquisition of Cuba by the United States. Territorially and commercially it would, in our hands, be an extremely valuable possession. Under certain contingencies it might be almost essential to our safety. Still, for domestic reasons, on which, in a communication of this kind, it might not be proper to dwell, the President thinks that the incorporation of the island into the Union at the present time, although effected with the consent of Spain, would be a hazardous measure; and he would consider its acquisition by force, except in a just war with Spain (should an event so greatly to be deprecated take place), as a disgrace to the civilization of the age.

The President has given ample proof of the sincerity with which he holds these views. He has thrown the whole force of his constitutional power against all illegal attacks upon the island. It would have been perfectly easy for him, without any seeming neglect of duty, to allow projects of a formidable character to gather strength by connivance. No amount of obloquy at home, no embarrassments caused by the indiscretions of the colonial government of Cuba, have moved him from the path of duty in this respect. The Captain-General of that island, an officer apparently of upright and conciliatory character, but probably more used to military command than the management of civil affairs, has, on a punctilio in reference to the purser of a private steamship (who seems to have been entirely innocent of the matters laid to his charge), refused to allow passengers and the mails of the United States to be landed from a vessel having him on board. This is certainly a very extraordinary mode of animadverting upon a supposed abuse of the liberty of the press by the subject of a foreign government in his native country. The Captain-General is not permitted by his government, three thousand miles off, to hold any diplomatic intercourse with the United States. He is subject in no degree to the direction of the Spanish minister at Washington ; and the President has to choose between a resort to force, to compel the abandonment of this gratuitous interruption of commercial intercourse (which would result in war), and a delay of weeks and months, necessary for a negotiation with Madrid, with all the chances of the most deplorable occurrences in the interval—and all for a trifle, that ought to have admitted a settlement by an exchange of notes between Washington and Havana. The President has, however, patiently submitted to these evils, and has continued faithfully to give to Cuba the advantages of those principles of the public law under the shelter of which she has departed, in this case, from the comity of nations. But the incidents to which I allude and which are still in train, are among many others which point decisively to the expediency of some change in the relations of Cuba; and the President thinks that the influence of France and England with Spain would be well employed in inducing her so to modify the administration of the government of Cuba as to afford the means of some prompt remedy for evils of the kind alluded to, which have done much to increase the spirit of unlawful enterprise against the island.

That a convention such as proposed would be a transitory arrangement, sure to be swept away by the irresistible tide of affairs in a new country, is, to the apprehension of the President, too obvious to require a labored argument. The project rests on principles applicable, if at all, to Europe, where international relations are, in their basis, of great antiquity, slowly modified, for the most part, in the progress of time and events; and not applicable to America, which, but lately a waste, is filling up with intense rapidity, and adjusting on natural principles those territorial relations which, on the first discovery of the continent, were in a good degree fortuitous.

The comparative history of Europe and America,

even for a single century, shows this. In 1752, France, England, and Spain were not materially different in their political position in Europe from what they now are. They were ancient, mature, consolidated states, established in their relations with each other and the rest of the world—the leading powers of Western and Southern Europe. Totally different was the state of things in America. The United States had no existence as a people; a line of English colonies, not numbering much over a million of inhabitants, stretched along the coast. France extended from the Bay of St. Lawrence to the Gulf of Mexico, and from the Alleghanies to the Mississippi; beyond which, westward, the continent was a wilderness, occupied by wandering savages, and subject to a conflicting and nominal claim on the part of France and Spain. Everything in Europe was comparatively fixed; everything in America provisional, incipient, and temporary, except the law of progress, which is as organic and vital in the youth of states as of individual men. A struggle between the provincial authorities of France and England for the possession of a petty stockade at the confluence of the Monongahela and Alleghany, kindled the seven-years war; at the close of which, the great European powers, not materially affected in their relations at home, had undergone astonishing changes on this continent. France had disappeared from the map of America, whose inmost recesses had been penetrated by her zealous missionaries and her resolute and gallant adventurers; England had added the Canadas to her trans-Atlantic dominions; Spain had become the mistress of Louisiana, so that, in the language of the archbishop of Mexico, in 1770, she claimed Siberia as the northern boundary of New Spain.

Twelve years only from the treaty of Paris elapsed, and another great change took place, fruitful of still greater changes to come. The American revolution broke out. It involved France, England, and Spain in a tremendous struggle; and at its close the United States of America had taken their place in the family of nations. In Europe, the ancient states were restored substantially to their former equilbrium; but a new element, of incalculable importance in reference to territorial arrangements, is henceforth to be recognized in America.

Just twenty years from the close of the war of the American revolution, France, by a treaty with Spain —of which the provisions have never been disclosed— possessed herself of Louisiana, but did so only to cede it to the United States; and in the same year, Lewis and Clark started on their expedition to plant the flag of the United States on the shores of the Pacific. In 1819, Florida was sold by Spain to the United States, whose territorial possessions in this way had been increased three-fold in half a century. This last acquisition was so much a matter of course that it had been

15

distinctly foreseen by the Count Aranda, then Prime Minister of Spain, as long ago as 1783.

But even these momentous events are but the forerunners of new territorial revolutions still more stupendous. A dynastic struggle between the Emperor Napoleon and Spain, commencing in 1808, convulsed the Peninsula. The vast possessions of the Spanish crown on this continent—vice-royalties and captain-generalships, filling the space between California and Cape Horn—one after another, asserted their independence. No friendly power in Europe, at that time, was able, or, if able, was willing, to succor Spain, or aid her to prop the crumbling buttresses of her colonial empire. So far from it, when France, in 1823, threw an army of one hundred thousand men into Spain to control her domestic politics, England thought it necessary to counteract the movement by recognizing the independence of the Spanish provinces in America. In the remarkable language of the distinguished minister of the day, in order to redress the balance of power in Europe, he called into existence a New World in the West—somewhat overrating, perhaps, the extent of the derangement in the Old World, and not doing full justice to the position of the United States in America, or their influence on the fortunes of their sister republics on this continent.

Thus, in sixty years from the close of the seven-years war, Spain, like France, had lost the last remains of her once imperial possessions on this continent. The United States, meantime, were, by the arts of peace, and the healthful progress of things, rapidly enlarging their dimensions and consolidating their power. The great march of events still went on. Some of the new republics, from the effect of a mixture of races, or the want of training in liberal institutions, showed themselves incapable of self-government. The province of Texas revolted from Mexico by the same right by which Mexico revolted from Spain. At the memorable battle of San Jacinto, in 1836, she passed the great ordeal of nascent States, and her independence was recognized by this government, by France, by England, and other European powers. Mainly peopled from the United States, she sought naturally to be incorporated into the Union. The offer was repeatedly rejected by Presidents Jackson and Van Buren, to avoid a collision with Mexico. At last the annexation took place. As a domestic question, it is no fit subject for comment in a communication to a foreign minister; as a question of a public law, there never was an extension of territory more naturally or justifiably made. It produced a disturbed relation with the government of Mexico; war ensued, and in its results other extensive territories were for a large pecuniary compensation on the part of the United States, added to the Union. Without adverting to the divisions of opinion which rose in refer-

17

ence to this war, as must always happen in free countries in reference to great measures, no person surveying these events with the eye of a comprehensive statesmanship can fail to trace in the main result the undoubted operation of the law of our political existence. The consequences are before the world. Vast provinces, which had languished for three centuries under the leaden sway of a stationary system, are coming under the influences of an active civilization. Freedom of speech and the press, the trial by jury, religious equality, and representative government, have been carried by the constitution of the United States into extensive regions in which they were unknown before. By the settlement of California, the great circuit of intelligence round the globe is completed. The discovery of the gold of that region—leading, as it did, to the same discovery in Australia—has touched the nerves of industry throughout the world. Every addition to the territory of the American Union has given homes to European destitution and gardens to European want. From every part of the United Kingdom, from France, from Switzerland and Germany, and from the extremest north of Europe, a march of immigration has been taken up, such as the world has never seen before. Into the United States—grown to their present extent in the manner described—but little less than half a million of the population of the Old World is annually pouring, to be immediately incorporated into an industrious and prosperous community, in the bosom of which they find political and religious liberty, social position, employment, and bread. It is a fact which would defy belief, were it not the result of official inquiry, that the immigrants to the United States from Ireland alone, besides having subsisted themselves, have sent back to their kindred, for the three last years, nearly five millions of dollars annually; thus doubling in three years the purchase-money of Louisiana.

Such is the territorial development of the United States in the past century. Is it possible that Europe can contemplate it with an unfriendly or jealous eye? What would have been her condition in these trying years but for the outlet we have furnished for her starving millions?

Spain, meantime, has retained of her extensive dominions in this hemisphere but the two islands of Cuba and Porto Rico. A respectful sympathy with the fortunes of an ancient ally and a gallant people, with whom the United States have ever maintained the most friendly relations, would, if no other reason existed, make it our duty to leave her in the undisturbed possession of this little remnant of her mighty trans-Atlantic empire. The President desires to do so; no word or deed of his will ever question her title or shake her possession. But can it be expected to last very long? Can it resist this mighty current in the fortunes of the world? Is it desirable that it should do so?

Can it be for the interest of Spain to cling to a possession that can only be maintained by a garrison of twenty-five or thirty thousand troops, a powerful naval force, and an annual expenditure for both arms of the service of at least twelve millions of dollars? Cuba, at this moment, costs more to Spain than the entire naval and military establishments of the United States costs the federal government. So far from being really injured by the loss of the island, there is no doubt that, were it peacefully transferred to the United States, a prosperous commerce between Cuba and Spain, resulting from ancient associations and common language and tastes, would be far more productive than the best contrived system of colonial taxation. Such, notoriously, has been the result to Great Britain of the establishment of the independence of the United States. The decline of Spain from the position which she held in the time of Charles the Fifth is coeval with the foundation of her colonial system; while within twenty-five years, and since the loss of most of her colonies, she has entered upon a course of rapid improvement, unknown since the abdication of that emperor.

I will but allude to an evil of the first magnitude : I mean the African slave-trade, in the suppression of which France and England take a lively interest—an evil which still forms a great reproach upon the civilization of Christendom, and perpetuates the barbarism of Africa, but for which, it is to be feared, there is no hope of a complete remedy while Cuba remains a Spanish colony.

But, whatever may be thought of these last suggestions, it would seem impossible for any one who reflects upon the events glanced at in this note to mistake the law of American growth and progress, or think it can be ultimately arrested by a convention like that proposed. In the judgment of the President, it would be as easy to throw a dam from Cape Florida to Cuba, in the hope of stopping the flow of the gulf stream, as to attempt, by a compact like this, to fix the fortunes of Cuba "now and for hereafter;" or, as expressed in the French text of the convention, "for the present as for the future," (pour le present comme pour l'avenir,) that is, for all coming time. The history of the past— of the recent past—affords no assurance that twenty years hence France or England will even wish that Spain should retain Cuba; and a century hence, judging of what will be from what has been, the pages which record this proposition will, like the record of the family compact between France and Spain, have no interest but for the antiquary.

Even now the President cannot doubt that both France and England would prefer any change in the condition of Cuba to that which is most to be apprehended, viz.: an internal convulsion which should renew the horrors and the fate of San Domingo.

I will intimate a final objection to the proposed

convention. M. de Turgot and Lord Malmesbury put forward, as the reason for entering into such a compact, "the attacks which have lately been made on the island of Cuba by lawless bands of adventurers from the United States, with the avowed design of taking possession of that island." The President is convinced that the conclusion of such a treaty, instead of putting a stop to these lawless proceedings, would give a new and powerful impulse to them. It would strike a death-blow to the conservative policy hitherto pursued in this country toward Cuba. No administration of this government, however strong in the public confidence in other respects, could stand a day under the odium of having stipulated with the great powers of Europe, that in no future time, under no change of circumstances, by no amicable arrangement with Spain, by no act of lawful war (should that calamity unfortunately occur), by no consent of the inhabitants of the island, should they, like the possessions of Spain on the American continent, succeed in rendering themselves independent; in fine, by no over-ruling necessity of self-preservation should the United States make the acquisition of Cuba.

For these reasons, which the President has thought it advisable, considering the importance of the subject, to direct me to unfold at some length, he feels constrained to decline respectfully the invitation of France and England to become parties to the proposed convention. He is pursuaded that these friendly powers will not attribute this refusal to any insensibility on his part to the advantages of the utmost harmony between the great maritime States on a subject of such importance. As little will Spain draw any unfavorable inference from this refusal; the rather, as the emphatic disclaimer of any designs against Cuba on the part of this government, contained in the present note, affords all the assurance which the President can constitutionally, or to any useful purpose, give, of a practical concurrence with France and England in the wish not to disturb the possession of that island by Spain.

I avail myself, sir, of this opportunity to assure you of my distinguished consideration.

EDWARD EVERETT.

www.ingramcontent.com/pod-product-compliance
Lightning Source LLC
Chambersburg PA
CBHW030915260626
47169CB00008B/2860